Eddie
the
Underdog

Dominic Purpura

Illustrations by Blueberry Illustrations

This book is dedicated to the man who gave me this game, taught me love, and exemplified hard work. To the greatest man, best friend, and father a kid could ever ask for:

Thank you for always believing in me, even when I didn't believe in myself. Thank you for giving everything you had to see me succeed. Thank you for endlessly sacrificing. Thank you for being at every game. Thank you for never allowing me to say "I give up." Thank you for loving my teammates and coaches. No matter how much time will pass between us, I will never forget all the ways I can thank you.

I love you forever, Dad.

Dom

I'm Eddie. That's me at bat.

I'm a baseball player! It was always
my favorite sport in the entire world.

There's something so great about running bases, catching the
ball, and swinging the bat. I could play the game forever!

There was just one problem ...

"STRIKE THREE, YOU'RE OUT!"

I was not very good.

In fact, I was the worst player on the team.

"Thanks, Eddie, we lost the game because
of you!" Porky was always reminding me.

It was true. We lost the game because of me. I felt like I was
the worst baseball player in history, but I didn't understand why!

I practiced every day and did the little things right,
and I worked extra hard when we'd play games.

But no matter what, I was just not very good at baseball.

If only I could be the great Beagle Ruth or Barry Bones ...
if only I was someone else ... I wouldn't be so bad.

"How'd the game go?" Mom asked as I walked inside.

"Horrible! I'm still the worst player," I said.

I grabbed my bat and baseball mitt and went outside to practice some more. They always said practice would make me better, but so far it wasn't working. Maybe I'm just not supposed to play.

"I don't know if I will ever be good. I should just quit," I said to my mom feeling sad.

"Well, before you decide to quit, can you go up to the attic and grab me a box of decorations?" Mom asked.

How strange! I was never allowed to go into the attic before, but I decided to go because practice wouldn't help anyways.

Cough, cough! It sure was dusty up here.

I looked through the boxes.

"Ouch!"

I kicked an old box.

It was Grandpa Eddie's box! I was named after him because he was one of the best baseball players in the town. Except, all I had was his name. I didn't have his talent.

The box opened on its own, and on the top was a letter that said,

To Eddie: My Grandson

Wait a minute, that's me!

Sell your books at sellbackyourBook.com!
Go to sellbackyourBook.com and get an instant price quote. We even pay the shipping - see what your old books are worth today!

Inspected By: Maria_DelRocio

00052362124

0005236 **2124** S

00052362124

Dear Eddie,

*I hope you are having a wonderful time playing baseball.
I remember when I was a pup, I was the worst player in the world.
No matter how much I practiced, I would never get better.*

*Until one day I learned something. I trained at swinging the bat,
catching the ball, and running bases. But none of those things work
unless you train your thoughts too. If I believed I was the worst
player, then I really was. The day before I gave up, I tried
to believe in myself first, and I hit my first home run!*

*Don't give up! Always believe and remember: You are
the best baseball player—if you believe it, you can be!*

*Sincerely,
Grandpa Eddie*

"Eddie! Where are you? Want to practice?" Dad was home.

I tucked the letter inside my pocket and ran downstairs.

Grandpa Eddie was right. I could practice every day doing the stuff on the outside, but I also needed to *train my thoughts* on the inside.

"Alright, Eddie. Here comes the ball," said Dad.

I stood there with the bat, and my dad pulled back to throw.

I started to think about how much I practiced, and how much I wanted to be better. Perhaps, I am not the worst baseball player after all.

SMACK!

The ball went flying out of the yard!

Maybe I can be good someday!

I *was* good at baseball! I *am* good at baseball!
All it took was a bit of practice both outside *and* inside.

I told myself this every day before
practice and every time I took to the field!

As the season started, I was getting better and better!

Finally, we made it all the way to the championship.

The game was tied with two of my teammates on the
bases and it came down to me, Eddie, at bat.

"Oh, no. We are going to lose!" Porky grumbled.

Before, I might have believed him. Instead,
I opened the letter and reread it one last time.

"I am a good player. I won't give up."

"STRIKE ONE!" the umpire shouted.

Suddenly, those negative thoughts of failure came back.
I thought maybe Grandpa's letter wasn't true!

"STRIKE TWO!"

"Oh, no!"

"I *am* a great player. I will *never* give up!" I shouted out loud.

I was going to be the best player because I *believed* I could be better, maybe even the best.

"I *am* a great player. I will *never* give up!"

I saw the pitcher pull back and get ready to throw.

I tightened my grip on the bat.

The ball came flying toward me, faster than ever.

I *can* hit the ball.

WHACK!

My first home run!

I really was a good player!

"And now, let's welcome the newest player. He is the most valuable player of the team and currently holds the record for the most home runs in one season. Here he is, Eddie the Underdog!"

I'm Eddie. That's me at bat.

I'm a baseball player! It is my favorite sport in the entire world. There is something so great about running bases, catching the ball, and swinging the bat. I could play the game forever!

And because I believe in myself, I know I will.

The end ... *for now*.

Dominic Purpura is a former 1st Team Mountain West All-Conference baseball player from San Diego State University (SDSU). Growing up in the small town of Hinsdale, Illinois, Dominic had a wild ride making it to the Division 1 level playing for his dream school. With zero offers out of his high school (Nazareth Academy), he attended Carthage College, a small Division 3 school in Kenosha, Wisconsin. He then transferred to Orange Coast College in Costa Mesa, California, where his team won two national titles. Soon, Dominic received more than 15 Division 1 offers and chose to play for San Diego State. After his two years at SDSU, he managed to work his way into the role of a starting pitcher, despite throwing what most people would think of as "way too slow." Dominic said the key to winning is having an "underdog mindset," no matter what the situation is. He is so grateful and thankful for the amazing coaches and teammates he was blessed to know over his journey. He believes most of his success can be attributed only to the countless amazing teammates and coaches he had fighting along his side. Without them, nothing would be possible. Lastly, he is endlessly grateful for the sacrifices his parents made for him, allowing him the opportunity to pursue his dream of playing Division 1 baseball.

For more details about the author and his work, please visit dompurpura.com.

Made in the USA
Las Vegas, NV
18 July 2022

51806972R00017